RANDOM Thoughts

VERONICA ATANANTE KUNG

ReadersMagnet, LLC

Random Thoughts
Copyright © 2020 by Veronica Atanante Kung

Published in the United States of America
ISBN Paperback: 978-1-952896-46-0
ISBN eBook: 978-1-952896-47-7

All rights reserved. No part of this publication may be reproduced, stored in a retrieval system or transmitted in any way by any means, electronic, mechanical, photocopy, recording or otherwise without the prior permission of the author except as provided by USA copyright law.

The opinions expressed by the author are not necessarily those of ReadersMagnet, LLC.

ReadersMagnet, LLC
10620 Treena Street, Suite 230 | San Diego, California, 92131 USA
1.619.354.2643 | www.readersmagnet.com

Book design copyright © 2020 by ReadersMagnet, LLC. All rights reserved.
Cover design by Ericka Obando
Interior design by Shemaryl Tampus

CONTENTS

Introduction vii

How to use this book ix

Random Thoughts 1

Saturday, January 26, 2019 5

Tuesday, January 29, 2019 7

Friday, January 31, 2019 8

Sunday, February 2, 2019. 9

Sunday, February 10, 2019. 11

Sunday, February 17, 2019 12

Thursday, February 21, 2019 13

Friday, February 22, 2019 15

Saturday, March 2, 2019 17

Monday, March 4, 2019 18

Saturday, March 9, 2019. 19

Wednesday, March 13, 2019 20

Friday, March 15, 2019 21

Sunday, March 17, 2019 22

Friday, March 22, 2019 23

Saturday, March 23, 2019 25

Wednesday, March 27, 2019 27

Thursday, March 28, 2019 28

Sunday, March 31, 2019. 30

INTRODUCTION

Random Thoughts was originally written as a book of non-fiction but I have found it to be between fiction and non-fiction. Thoughts were written based on events I have encountered and those that I have created. I wanted to share only the thoughts based on facts but found that I also could be creative when I wrote.

I wrote this book, in a sense, as my "self-help" book. A book where I would write on certain days to help me get through the day. I suffer from schizoaffective disorder. This disorder has many avenues and I chose to share the thoughts that lead me to as much as possible a normal life. In my particular disorder, I can feel a lot of anxiety and worry that cause me to react physically to muscle movements that I have no control over - especially obsessive compulsive movements of my tongue and jaw. It is embarrassing when this happens outside of my home because I feared judgement by people that they would judge that there was something weirdly wrong with me. I felt this way for a time.

One day my psychiatrist told me, "No one can help you. You must be vigilant and help yourself." This remained unclear in my thoughts until 27 years later. I learned that I love expressing my thoughts through writing. I remember that as a 9-year-old, I began journaling with letters to God. I stopped at the age of 16-years-old and, encouraged by my dear sister and mother, to journal again in the 1990s. One day, I just opened up a new journal my sister gifted me and wrote.

By July 2019, I wanted to share my thoughts on how I found my way to lead as much as possible a normal life. Holly Worton, an author I came across, who is a member of the Druid order OBOD, also wrote a book. She found trees communicating their wisdom to her. I wrote about God and found Him listening to me.

HOW TO USE THIS BOOK

I am just passing on the message on how books can be read. Like a couple of books I have read, you may choose to read the whole book (since it is short) in chronological order, the way I wrote it. Or, you may choose to open the book to a day's thought and read it that way. Or, you may choose to read a day at a time like a devotional. When you read, you can choose to stop at any time and continue another day. You may find some thoughts useful and other thoughts not so useful. After reading the entire book, you may choose to re-read it to remind yourself that a day can always get better. There is no definite way on how to read this book. It is up to your choice. I like the way Holly Worton, puts it, *you do you.*

I hope this book helps you contemplate on how it may relate to your daily life experiences. This is my way of coping with mood disorder in my life. In this book, I refer to God whispering to me a lot. That is my big picture, God is in my life. He transforms my thoughts and helps me along life. I hope that when you read, you further put thought into the big picture that is your life, and work on doing the best you can in your mental illness. You may choose to follow my path, or you may find a better way of getting out of misery and anxiety and times of constant unkind thoughts. God fills this world with graces for you to come across and experience the magnanimity of this world created for you. Perhaps, one day you might want to share your experiences and journal; maybe, even become a published author.

Life is too short to succumb to schizoaffective disorder. I have found my way to cope. Thank you, Lord, for this beautiful day.

I would like to dedicate this book
to four persons in my life whom have
encouraged and supported me to write my way into
an appreciation of my life -
Iana, Felix, Teresa and Monina

RANDOM THOUGHTS

This is a story among stories I have in my head. These are my day by day short thoughts of how I think and what makes my complete thought for the day. This story is driven with the hope that my writing will give an avenue for people who suffer with schizoaffective disorder.

I come from a childhood with much solitude. My only friend was God. I would spend memorable times kneeling and praying by my mom's bedside, and writing to God in my kid diary. God was my best friend because He always listened to me, even when I complained in my solitude because of anger.

I wrote at the age of twelve:

Dear Lord,

When something goes wrong, why does it always have to be me crying and hurt? I am sure my siblings have seen me cry because my mother always scolds me. Always me! I surely haven't seen my sister cry because she was scolded. Sometimes I really pretend she is not my sister.

Every time I do something wrong, she does not do anything but tell mum. I always fight for myself, not like her.

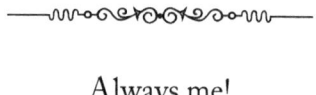

Always me!

My thoughts were fragmented and lacked coherence, but for sure I often strongly disliked myself. Sometimes, I would deface pages in my diary because of anger resulting from solitude. I would write angry words over a page from the past. I was angry with my life as it twisted and twirled inside of me. I was unhappy. But after all that anger in my writing, God was still there for me. He blessed me along the way with a child.

I made promises, like that I would bring her up in the way I learned how a child should be brought up—without solitude.

In solitude, my speech lacked coherence. Hence, I always encouraged my daughter to communicate well. Now, when she is angered, she is able to describe her feelings, which enables me to understand how to help her not withdraw from God for long periods of time. In addition, she developed skills to be empathetic toward others, so when she meets other children, through good communication, she finds good friends. When she experiences feelings of loneliness, she uses words to express herself and is able to easily make friends wherever there is a gathering. Communicating well has brought many other blessings and a few good friends, alleviating her from solitude.

Being successful in her relationships, she has thanked God with sincerity, and so have I. I am so glad I began writing and found God listening. I can often reflect on how life was as I was growing up to help my daughter to become the best version of herself.

For me personally, writing has helped me with focusing on life with my child and is helping in my mental disorder. And, it just so happens that my vocation in my life is my family. Writing opens up many avenues to many genres, and like my child taught me, a pizza can be eaten with a fork and a knife. Pizza can be eaten with bare hands, too. Or, even chopsticks can be used to eat pizza.

What I am trying to say is that one has to find his or her own way that helps his or her mental disorder. This is my way of dealing with my mental illness.

This begins on:

Saturday, January 26, 2019
It's 9:09 p.m.

Today is a beautiful day, is what I should have started off with in my head this morning, but that is not what I did. As I write this evening, I feel sorry. I should remember this every morning and say a thank you to our Lord for this beautiful day. I would have been smiling as I drove to Taekwondo class with my daughter. The sun would have shone on my face from a warm, clear sky. Down the road, we would not have driven bothered with a red traffic light stopping us in our tracks.

If I had started off with how beautiful a day it was and thanked God, I would already have been singing, "Alleluia,

alleluia," down the street toward the church. My unstylish hairdo would not have bothered me. An empty stomach would not have bothered me. I would have been set up to conquer the day and had the time of my life as I drove to the Taekwondo class, which started at ten in the morning. I would not have needed a twelve oz. coffee to cure my craving.

Today is a beautiful day, is what I will say tomorrow morning and every morning after that.

Tuesday, January 29, 2019
It's 7:34 p.m.

Thank you, Lord, for this beautiful day.

"You should never talk bad about your sister because she is your sister and your own blood. If you need to talk, don't talk to your spouse about it, but talk to grandma because she is your sister and your own blood."

Friday, January 31, 2019
It's 9:05 p.m.

Thank you, Lord, for this beautiful day. Oh Lord, the wonderful things that You put into my mind. There is hope for me to get married in church under the eyes of God. My ears, almost shut to the despair of no options, were forcibly opened by a Carmelite friar at the possible chance of getting my husband's annulment approved by the archdiocese. I smiled from ear to ear, and my thoughts expounded. All I had to do was contact the archdiocese and ask if my husband could produce another witness and if I could approach my husband's sister and explain to her that her testimony will not cause the other children to become illegitimate. Her misunderstanding of the process could put rest in her mind that the archdiocese is only looking for the loss of sacraments in his previous marriage, making his ties annullable. God will make me whole again with this one conversation that will change my family's lineage like that of Ruth in the Bible, whose decision to stay with Naomi ensured the lineage to the family of Jesse and King David and to Jesus.

Sunday, February 2, 2019
It's 7:23 p.m.

Thank you, Lord, for this beautiful day. Every day, no matter how stale it seems, I will thank the Lord for a beautiful day. Today was not an unusual Sunday, except it was pouring cats and dogs. Driving home from Taekwondo practice, this was my thought…I was silent. I didn't know what to say. I thought, being that it was a quarter 'til five, I would be on time for Mass. I had tremendous doubts that my husband and Hannah would attend Mass with me. It had been a while. With the virtue of courage, I asked, "Will you two come to church with me?"

Hannah said, "I have to change first." The weather was too cold for her to stay in her Taekwondo uniform. I acknowledged gratefully. My husband said nothing, and I was content. My heart was lifted because I knew what that meant…I said nothing, nothing at all, but thanked him in my mind, heart, and soul that he did not decline to go to Mass with us. God is so gracious. This made me more in love with my husband. After Father Philip motioned the parishioners to greet each other, I kissed my husband on the cheek and greeted him with a blessing that peace be with him. This joy I received today lasted through a hot, home-cooked meal and the rest of the day.

Sunday, February 10, 2019
It's 8:21 p.m.

Thank you, Lord, for this beautiful day. You have given me insight into my thinking today. Most people have to go through life lessons and learn from the experience. You have granted me many life lessons to learn from, yet I had never had a child nor been related to other children much when I was younger. Yet, You grant me wondrous advice to bring up my daughter. Oh, how I am humbled. I do not deserve You to be under my roof, yet You are always there, guiding me through, bringing untainted, unresearched facts for a child like me, with schizoaffective disorder and much memory loss, to think. I pray these thoughts will always be Your will as I bring up my daughter with wisdom daily.

Sunday, February 17, 2019
It's 11:38 a.m.

Thank you, Lord, for this beautiful morning. My fruit juice is sweet. Why is fruit juice made even sweeter by adding additional sugar to juice concentrate? "That's so much sugar," as quoted by my sister.

Life is already sweet. Why are there additional pleasures added to it? Isn't life sweet enough? Why do I feel like I need to have that sweet and fizzy bubbly water?

Teresa Kung and Veronica Kung

Thursday, February 21, 2019
It's 12:20 p.m.

Thank you, Lord, for this beautiful morning.

One thing I have learned is to speak highly to a child. Mei Lin is going to be a great woman. I texted her mom that she has her parents and brother and relatives to bring her there.

Another thing I have learned is to save my daughter's emotions. Earlier on when I picked her up from school, I said that to my daughter without really knowing what I meant. I just felt the need to say it, along with the warm feeling of God in my thoughts telling me to say it. I tried to explain it to her.

I wanted to save her emotions. She added, "Parents get angry when their children call them up to be picked up from school." The children were often a little under the weather.

I told her, "I am glad you called me." She had a pinching pain in her upper left liver area. We got home, warmed up some canned soup and were sipping and munching Doritos on the side, and she was quite content. She was ravenous. My thoughts skipped a beat, and I suspected that she was having pain in what she called "her stomach" because she had a tiny ulcer in her stomach. It makes sense…does it not? Then while munching the chip and sucking the soup off the Chinese spoon, she added that sometimes when she is hungry, she does not eat. Bingo! That's it; she had some gastric acid giving a burning sensation in her stomach! I heard that milk helps.

So, parents quickly getting upset with their children does not solve the children's problem that they're feeling a little under the weather. Actually, it could make them more stressed to know that they don't know what's physically wrong with them, and their parents' anger could create non-beneficial emotions. Although my daughter could have been lost in so much confusion, I actually saved her emotions by telling her that I am glad she called and by listening to her describe her symptoms. It took a trip to Target and some cooking and good old mom-and-daughter chatting, but she and I felt we did the right thing.

Friday, February 22, 2019
It's 10:04 p.m.

Thank you, Lord, for this beautiful day. It always seems to be right to write when I am emotional.

We fought…my husband and I.

Even though we fought with some unforgivable words, like asking him why he has to be poor, I thank the Lord for this beautiful day.

…because I learned how much I loved my husband.

It's 10:23 p.m., after I fought with my spouse and wrote about how I thank the Lord for this beautiful day because I learned how much I loved my husband.

I was not upset and crying in the car at my spouse because he is poor. I said it to hurt him because he had hurt my feelings.

[Pause] I must love him, because I was open to listening and being counseled by my ten-year old daughter at a restaurant. "He just doesn't know how to take care of girls." She explained with concern. "He had four boys to bring up, and why do you think he broke off with the other woman?" was what I heard her saying. Hannah stirred up the loving feelings I had inside of me for her dad. With every ounce of her little being, she stirred up my longing to be reunited with peace and love.

[Pause] I had been angry with my husband because of problems lurking and pestering me inside myself—feelings of not being wanted, feelings of ugliness, feelings of not being appreciated, feelings of lacking in goal-setting.

I love my spouse so much. This evening, I wanted him to be all that lacked in my psyche. Now, all I wanted was to reunite with him with peace and love. I understand that this is not humanly possible and that only God can fulfill needs in me. "Oh, Jesus! Meek and humble heart. Hear me…from the desire of being approved. Deliver me, Jesus," I prayed.

All these feelings are answered by the one line of the Litany of Humility, but the feeling of lack in goal-setting isn't.

This can be easily Googled, I thought, and so I did; I Googled.

Then on my cell popped up an article about goal-directed behavior in schizophrenia patients.

Saturday, March 2, 2019
It's 5:39 p.m.

Thank you, Lord, for the beautiful day. I am lost today. I have no goals in my head. I have no energy in my body. I am not interested in the news about our president. I have no idea what is wrong with me. And yet, I can see the world going on. My husband massages my injured father. He very patiently stays with me at my father's home. My brother thanks my husband for his services. My daughter constantly asks if I am okay. She spends the day painting seashells in brilliant colors. My mom asks me how I am feeling. My husband doesn't want to get paid for massaging my father because he is doing it out of the kindness of his heart.

This is what I am thankful for. The world continues around me with love for others, kindness to others, gratitude toward others, and care for others.

Monday, March 4, 2019
It's 5:46 a.m.

Reverend Father most holy,

That it may come to pass that we love those who loathe us, so that we may be strengthened in our hearts to love You, Father.

May this Lenten season bring us to turn to You more than ever.

Pax.

Saturday, March 9, 2019
It's 8:06 p.m.

Thank you, Lord, for this beautiful day. Today, I felt comforted to be understood by my daughter and my friend, Hellen.

I had been glum all week, and after taking the medicine (Chinese herbs) for two days, I found the courage to intervene my negative thoughts—courage that was always subdued by depression but always there as a gift from God. At moments, it was tempting to start negative thinking and talking, but I said, "No! No more!"

Wednesday, March 13, 2019
It's 9:07 p.m.

Lord, my heart is torn. What is torture? Where am I in my life? I am confused.

I trust You. I believe in You. I will not give up,

because I am Your warrior. Lord, be my shield…be my guide. I love You to the moon and back.

Friday, March 15, 2019
It's 8:22 p.m.

Thank you, Lord, for this beautiful day.

Sunday, March 17, 2019
It's 10:05 a.m.

One day, Hannah will see the things I do that make me cry and know that when I cry, I am happy. Things that make me cry touch my heart as though God was giving me a transfusion of what He holds deep in His heart. That is humanity and love.

I enjoyed watching the movie *Little Notes to Heaven* by Cody and Carl Hallford.

It's 10:12 p.m.

Jesus, I offer this day to You. This is now my morning offering to You. Thank you, Lord, for this beautiful day.

Friday, March 22, 2019
It's 8:15 p.m.

Thank you, Lord, for this beautiful day. More than twice, I have lost confidence and believed that I was a bad mother and wife because I had gotten sick so often. Yesterday, I heard a little voice in my head that said I am trying my best and there is no bad or good because each and every one of us is unique. I have been through experiences in my life that were different than those of other mothers and wives to come to where I am now.

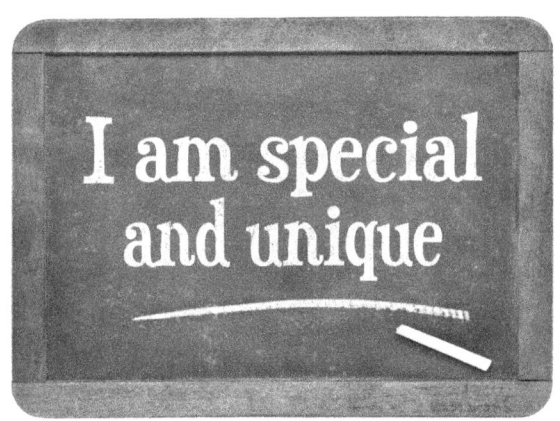

Uniqueness is a popular word commonly used in my family of three. It has always been a word that needs no conversation or explanation once said. Another way of putting it is one of a kind. There is no need to compare any other person because each child or husband is different—both needing a mother or wife and time to really know the other person, over time.

Saturday, March 23, 2019
It's 3:58 p.m.

Thank you, Lord, for this beautiful early afternoon. Praise be to Jesus Christ! An act of God's wisdom and God's encouragement happened today. I had just filled out the FACTS tuition assistance application for my daughter's school. As usual, after filling out the application, I was sad—sad with $16,000 in credit card and loan debt, and only $8,000 in the bank. Clearly, my family expenses were more than our liquidity.

My sadness quickly brought my husband's mood down too. He came close to ranting how we always needlessly spend too much. I had heard it before, and I just kept silent with my speech. However, in my head, I was arguing that the family would be okay if my husband had a better paying job with benefits and if he did not paddle so much. Paddling was his passion, and it took up almost his entire weekend. My mind was saying that he could be working another job to bring in more bread.

Yes, I was silent. Then, God kicked in. "Veronica, be strong and stand up for what you believe in handling your finances. Talk to your husband and comfort him with these words: 'God spoke to me and gave me wisdom. Did you ever think that I have not been using my credit cards?'"

I affirmed, picking positive words out of the ranting my husband made.

"You are right. Things are okay…We do not use our credit cards."

The atmosphere in the bedroom seemed calm. Relieved, my husband had nothing to say to accuse my daughter and I of needless spending. With clear thinking, the debt had already been there for a few months. With clear thinking, how is it that we are spending more without credit cards and loans? We are in a time where money is easy to borrow, but with good discipline, we have not borrowed. By faithfully paying monthly, the debt has actually gone down to $16,000.

Thank you, Lord, for whispering wisdom and encouragement into my head.

Wednesday, March 27, 2019
It's 7:23 p.m.

Thank you, Lord, for this beautiful day. I prayerfully begged and asked for peace of mind. I…got to thinking, *What is a good friend?* Just one very peaceful, fragmented day.

Thursday, March 28, 2019
It's 2:36 p.m.

In an email, I wrote.

Celine, yesterday I took time off because I was sick. Because of the nature of my illness, I could have come in in the afternoon, but as I will be using exempt time and you said that I have to make up my time if I use exempt time freely, I did not come in. I find your decision as an infringement upon my right to use exempt time.

I was sick and should be allowed to use exempt time without making up the time, like everyone else. If you were sick, would you not use exempt time? I was not using the time to do anything else that would prove that I was lying. I know you do not believe me, but my illness is very real and has no cure. Since my return to work full time, I have documented 99 percent of my absences. Unlike others, I have had to prove I was not using exempt time freely. You can refer to these online. If you still don't believe me, I am willing to come in and make up some and not all of the time, understanding this is a division requirement in my case. Please let me know which times you would like me to make up and that it is okay with Human Resources and Mark Blank.

Sunday, March 31, 2019
It's 6:30 p.m.

Thank you, Lord, for this beautiful day . . . What is a good friend?

"I am struggling today!" That's what I texted to my ladies. As usual, I ended up being the only one texting. I texted how my father was now in a wheelchair. Then to my surprise, my ladies texted back, and they talked about everything under *MY* sun, from discovering ducks in a park to hospice to a summary of my dad's love for me. By the end of the day, I was thanking the Lord for giving me not one but two good friends. They took time out of their busy family schedules to talk me through my sickness. Maybe they did not realize it, but God kept them with me while I was down.

Then there's my daughter, Hannah. At lunch, I was pretty down from raising my voice at my mother while we were in the park. So, my daughter talked me into having matcha green tea ice cream drinks at Tea Station. The restaurant was far, but we drove there anyway. Matcha sounded good. Pepping me or anyone up is a specialty of Hannah.

At the restaurant, to manage and challenge my struggling thoughts, she told me how I watch over her and all that. She was right.

She told me how she liked fish fillet and how she never knows the name of the dish but just calls it fish fillet. She made me smile crisply as she reminded me how she savored a favorite dish.

She even jolted my thoughts when she told me she liked 75 percent sugar in her Taro Snow Ice with boba drink. I always ordered her drink with no sugar. :)

My daughter is my gem. We finished off the day with miniature Japanese candy 'coca-cola' ramen. As I write, she's baking cupcakes for dinner, which I suspect are purple-colored!

Maybe she did not realize how she straightened my thoughts and substituted them with happy thoughts. She did so, so splendidly and naturally. I thank God for His gifts to her.

I thank God for His gifts of good friends and my oh-so-precious daughter to me.

So, here are some random thoughts that are typical of my mental illness. Much of the time, I am sad, but I've learned to cope by always thinking how God has made every day a beautiful day.

www.ingramcontent.com/pod-product-compliance
Lightning Source LLC
LaVergne TN
LVHW020446080526
838202LV00055B/5361